SC E Moore

Moore, Elaine.

Deep river /

Deep River

Deep River

by Elaine Moore
illustrated by Henri Sorensen

Simon & Schuster Books for Young Readers
Published by Simon & Schuster
New York • London • Toronto • Sydney • Tokyo • Singapore

*N*ight air bounces off the leaves outside my window.
It whispers through the curtains.

"We still goin', Jess?"

I sit up fast. Grandpa puts a finger to his lips. We're going
fishing. Just the two of us. Usually, it's my brother who goes
fishing with Grandpa. This is the first time for me.

Grandpa is wearing an old, wrinkled hat. Grandma says
it's as old as the hills. "Here, Jess." He tosses me a hat. "The
sun gets hot out there on the water."

We load up our gear and creep out, careful the screen
door doesn't slam behind us.

The moon's round dish-face makes a shimmery path to
Grandpa's truck. The stars are shiny pebbles lying so close to
the ground I could scoop them up with my hand. It is like
church, cool and quiet. Talking loud doesn't seem right.

Grandpa parks the truck and tilts his head to listen. Fishing-hole sounds: water lapping, tree frogs chirping, and Grandpa and me being quiet so we don't scare the fish.

"Come along, Jess," Grandpa whispers. "You can help me pull the boat from the thicket."

When Grandpa tells me, I climb into the boat. He hands me the rest of the gear.

"Sit now while I give her a shove."

When the boat rocks, I grab on to the sides. "Hurry, Grandpa!" I shout, forgetting how I might scare the fish.

With a cold splash, Grandpa scrambles inside. It will be my fault if we don't catch anything.

"Don't worry," Grandpa says, smiling. "There's more than one fish in this river. We couldn't have scared all of them."

Grandpa works the oars. He whistles to himself. I make a little rudder with my hand. I hum and try to forget what my brother told me about the bait.

"I don't like worms," I say.

"Didn't bring worms, Jess. Brought flies instead."

"Fishing flies. Right, Grandpa?"

Grandpa takes off his hat and carefully removes a sharp hook that has a dangling yellow lure.

"Yep. This here's a humdinger."

I watch Grandpa tie the humdinger neatly to my line. Then he flicks my rod back and forth. With a sharp snap the humdinger soars off like a bird and lands in the water.

"Here, Jessie." He hands me the rod. "Let me show you how." Grandpa sits beside me. He covers my hands with his. "Like this," he says as the rod bends backward and then forward.

"Simple, Grandpa."

Grandpa smiles. I smile, too. But when I try, the humdinger is a wet duck. It plops inside the boat. Next it's a bug snagging Grandpa's hat. I bet Grandpa wishes he'd brought my brother instead of me!

But Grandpa only laughs. "Guess it takes some getting used to," he says.

Finally, the humdinger flips into the water, making ripples so bright I have to shade my eyes.

Grandpa makes a low whistle. "Fine cast, Jess."

Now I'm sure I can catch a fish.

All morning, Grandpa and I drift and row. The sun spreads bright
yellow paint across the sky that spills into the water and winks at me.
But best is the way our rods sing when we cast off.

"Grandpa, I caught a log." If my brother were here, he would laugh
at me.

Grandpa gives my rod a sharp jerk. Like magic, the humdinger
snaps free.

"We'll go fishing for logs some other time," Grandpa says. "What do you think? Could we use a little shade while we eat lunch?" Grandpa takes off his hat and wipes his forehead with his arm. "Besides, fish don't bite much when it's hot."

Grandpa rows to a shady spot. We balance our sandwiches in our laps. I drink my soda with long, thirsty gulps while Grandpa sips his coffee from a tin cup. Afterward, we decide to stretch our legs in the woods.

"Are we going to catch any fish?" I ask Grandpa. My father and brother never come home empty-handed.

"Well, I tell you, Jess." Grandpa brushes the pine needles from his hat. "You have to be quick to catch a fish. When you get that first nibble, *bang*! you have to snap back fast or it'll get away. Sometimes you don't get a second chance."

"But I haven't gotten a tiny nibble, Grandpa. Maybe these fish don't like humdingers."

Grandpa grabs my arm. "Enough daydreaming! If the fish won't come to us, we'll go in after them!"

"How, Grandpa?"

Before I know it, Grandpa is pulling long rubber boots out of the boat. "Here, these waders will keep us dry!"

Grandpa sits down on the creek bank. He pulls his waders on first. Then he helps me with mine.

"They're too big, Grandpa. I might fall down." I don't want to tell Grandpa I'm afraid.

"That's what your brother said the first time, but you'll get used to them. And don't be put off when you cast. It's the same whether you're standing or sitting. Just remember everything I told you."

Grandpa hands me my rod. "We don't want to scare the fish with our footsteps."

"But, Grandpa, my waders sound like squeaky mice."

"*Shh!* Quiet mice, Jess."

Grandpa and I stalk the water's edge like two Indians. We are hiding from the fish. We're going to sneak up on them with our humdingers.

Grandpa signals. He's found the right spot. Quietly, we start down the bank. But when we get close to the water, it doesn't look like a shallow stream anymore. It has grown into a deep river.

Grandpa walks beside me. Into the cold, swirling water we go, just the two of us. The current swirls around my ankles. It pushes at my legs. The wind whips at my jacket.

I push the button down on my reel. I hold the rod up and back. "Just a tad," I remember Grandpa saying. I flick my wrist and the rod sings. The humdinger hops, pops, and skittles as it races downstream. *Click!* The line catches on my reel.

Suddenly, I feel a sharp tug.

"Grandpa, a fish! I caught a fish!"

I try to reel back quick, the way Grandpa said, but my rod jerks as the fish zooms back and forth. I can hardly hang on. Oh, no! I waited all day for this fish. What if it gets away? What if I drop Grandpa's rod? What if I lose the humdinger?

Grandpa's hand is on my shoulder.

"Hold your pole up. Stand firm. You can do it, Jess."

I reel and hold back. When I look up, a silvery fish dances on its tail.

"*Ya-hoooo!*"

Grandpa waits until I reel the fish close. Then he grabs my line, slides the net under the water, and scoops up the fish.

"Nice catch, Jess."

Grandpa gently backs the hook out of the fish's mouth. I can watch, but I wouldn't want to do it.

"Looks like a keeper, Jessie."

"Let me put it in the bucket, Grandpa."

I hold out my hands and the fish flops its tail. I jump and Grandpa laughs. My fish feels like any old slimy fish and it smells like stinky feet, but I'm still glad Grandpa said "keeper."

The rest of the afternoon, Grandpa and I take turns.

"Get the net, Jess!" Grandpa hollers. He snagged a whopper!

Simple. I remember how he slid the net under the water, smooth as silk.

"Use two hands, Jess! You can do it!"

I guess it takes some getting used to.

My brother says you have to be lucky to catch a fish. Mostly, I think you have to know how.

Finally, the fish go home. It's time for us to go home, too. I help Grandpa wrap up our catch. Afterward, we wash our hands in the river. I don't whistle like Grandpa. I hum quietly to myself.

It is a fishing song that has no words except inside my head, the song of Grandpa and me.

"Grandpa?"

Grandpa smiles. Instead of hooking the humdinger in his cap, he fastens it to mine. "Now it's your fishing hole, too," he says.

I tilt my head like Grandpa. All around, trees whisper.
Already I see a lightning bug.
    Grandpa and I will follow it home.

To Dad, Daddy, and Uncle Sylvester
—E.M.

To Martin, Marianne, and Per
—H.S.

SIMON & SCHUSTER BOOKS FOR YOUNG READERS
Simon & Schuster Building, Rockefeller Center
1230 Avenue of the Americas, New York, New York 10020
Text copyright © 1994 by Elaine Moore
Illustrations copyright © 1994 by Henri Sorensen
Designed by David Neuhaus.
The text of this book was set in 15 point Berkeley Old
Style Medium. The illustrations were done in acrylic.
Manufactured in the United States of America
10 9 8 7 6 5 4 3 2 1
Library of Congress Cataloging-in-Publication Data
Moore, Elaine. Deep river/by Elaine Moore; illustrated by Henri Sorensen.
p. cm. Summary: On their first fishing trip together, Grandpa and Jess
try to catch a whopper. [1. Fishing—Fiction. 2. Grandfathers—Fiction.]
I. Sorensen, Henri, ill. II. Title. PZ7.M7832De 1994 [E]—dc20 93–23043 CIP
ISBN: 0–671–87278–8